THE COMPANY WE KEEP

PAUSE

Lisa M. Harrien

All Rights Reserved. No part of this publication may be reproduced in any form or by any means, including scanning, photocopying, or otherwise without prior written permission of the copyright holder. Copyright © 2017

ACKNOWLEDGMENTS

The only being that deserves to be acknowledged is the Supreme Being, for without the positive energy, strength and guidance I welcomed and received I would not have been able to attain such heights as this.

THE TEA

As for the family and friends who kicked me while I was down, just as recently as last year, words cannot explain what I feel for you. Perhaps emptiness sums it up. Shewing you from my presence/mindset has done great things for me. If it had not been for your grave disappointments and capricious behavior I would still be interacting with spirits that were virulent to my soul. Good luck with that.

ABOUT THE AUTHOR

Me? Lil ole me? A seventies baby out of Detroit, Michigan born Lisa M. Mason, the eldest and only girl of five. Married twice (the first time was before I was 20 years old) doomed to fail. He and I have three children together (I had three by the time I was nineteen). Married again at about 28 years old, we grew apart but remain cordial. He and I have one child together. I chose nursing as my career path. Writing is my passion! I enjoy reading, traveling, shopping (as most girls/women), researching (just about anything), learning, among many other things. I am very adventurous. My personality in my opinion can be described as ZANY.

"Associate yourself with people of good quality, for it is better to be alone than in bad company."

BOOKER T. WASHINGTON

Feel free to follow me on IG @l_michele99 or authorl.harrien

Via FB @ Rayne Floods or authorl.harrien

Chain of Events

Introduction	1
Chapter 1	**9**
The Meet	11
The Meet Ii	25
Chapter 2	**32**
The Past	37
Reacquainting	40
Chapter 3	**44**
Devastation	50
Departure	53
Disgust And Despair	57
Chapter 4	**60**
Good Ole Fun	65
Chapter 5	**68**
The Beginning	75
Under Construction	85
Wedded Bliss	87
Long Awaited Tuesday	96

INTRODUCTION

In Michigan's history on rare occasions you could see snowfall in June/July and with that being said, you either love it, leave it or deal with it. I can remember steamy summers as a kid in Detroit aka "The Motor City," a swim mobile would come and park on Kitchener Street. Chaps from neighboring blocks would gather around and one by one, we would climb the little ladder attached to the truck, dive in and for hours we would splish and splash. Meanwhile, the air would smell like fresh cut grass and the Jackson Five or The Gap Band could be heard in the distance. The swim mobile would beat the adults turning on the hydrants for us to cool down because we'd have to stop playing in the water due to a car, bus or mail carrier driving along our street. If you stood too close to the opened valve of the hydrant, it would feel as if the pressure from the water would rip your skin clean off. Nonetheless, it was fun, but not as fun as the swim mobile.

I was born the oldest of two. My brother, a couple of years younger than I, departed this life as a child from complications of sickle cell disease. I miss him so very much. One of my fondest memories of him happened early one Easter morning. Momma and I woke up to find the triple layer German chocolate cake she baked missing half of its coconut icing and every colorful jelly bean atop was gone. Making his way from his bedroom down the stairs and into the dining room...my big-little brother oh about six years old was "dressed" in his sky-blue pin striped suit, the white shirt was not tucked in, and his vest was buttoned, just not properly. Poor kid looked sideways.

With remnants of the coconut icing on his face our mom asked him, "What happened to the cake baby?" His guilty yet enthusiastic response was, "The Easter bunny did it!!" Ma and I looked at one another and smiled then we laughed in unison. After getting past that early morning we attended church. The fun-filled festivities were great. There was the talent show followed by the Easter egg hunt. To top it off the best dinner at home that evening. Momma's cookin' is the absolute best! I can vividly remember sitting on the couch after dinner with my eyes slightly closed cradling my full belly while watching The Incredible Hulk and smiling...it was a good day. That's until I heard daddy yelling at Momma... he would do that often. My little brother Donovan ran and joined me on the couch. We whispered curse words to our daddy as he yelled at Momma. We were thick as thieves in a good way.

Football, football, football!! I don't know if Donovan could go a day without tossing one or watching a game whether it be amateur or pro. He would play this tabletop football game and the players would move across the board/field magnetically. Our neighbor Kevin would quarterback a football to my little brother in the middle of the street sometimes. If Donovan missed a toss Kevin would scream out, "RIGHT THROUGH THE ARMS!!" Our pappy hated the relationship between my brother and Kevin, I couldn't understand why because he barely gave us the time of day. Donovan played Pewee Football for a brief period. Momma had to withdraw him after finding out about his illness and that alone damn near killed him. Following the discovery of his diagnosis I would play his tabletop game and watch football games on television with him.

Growing up I was spoiled shitless and never wanted for anything. A chubby kid with caramel toned skin, hazel-grey eyes (four eyed), beyond shoulder length dark brown hair, pocket protector wearing all around nerd. Superb in school. My third-grade teacher Mr. Allen recommended that I be double promoted to the fifth grade. "Yall are not gonna have my baby around those big kids." I can remember thinking was…dang I'm as big if not bigger than most of 'em Momma! (rollin' my eyes within my thought). As if being chunky wasn't bad enough the awkward shape and the glasses did not help one bit. Throughout junior high I was called, "Four eyed flat booty Judy." Those same little fucks needed science and math tutoring lessons. They started begging to pay me for help. My favorite subject was science but throughout junior high I was on the equation team. We won several tournaments. I guess it's safe to say that being a math whiz made me geeky as well.

My Mom, Ella was born an identical twin. She is a very caring and tender- hearted individual that would give you her last. Her twin, Aunt Etta is ex-military honorably discharged and is now the owner of a small deli that sits between Detroit and Redford Township. Momma and Aunt Etta are red bones with freckles, hazel-grey eyed brunettes and stand about five feet ten inches tall them some thick sistas. They rarely hear from their brother Eddie III. All I can remember is a new born baby boy and a little girl cousin around my age and that Uncle Eddie left to follow his baby momma and moved to New York ... Momma nor Aunt Etta never speak of him and me...I don't ask.

My daddy with his no- good ass 'bout drove Momma crazy with his verbal and physical abuse. He ran around on her to. She had been severely depressed ever since the death of my lil brother. I think daddy blamed her to pacify his own ass. Everything in me wished she'd leave his sorry ass alone. During my first semester as a senior in high school, Momma had a stroke after daddy put his hands on her. I tried to whoop his ass! Depression, high blood pressure, diabetes and now this! I felt helpless for Momma. She went away and during that time Aunt Etta stepped in and looked after me. She had to rehabilitate from the stroke and then was transferred to a place for folks whose "minds are a lil sick," as Aunt Etta put it. I have no doubt that she will pull through.

While in the rehab facility Momma came home on the weekends and holidays. She was weak and although I hated it I knew she needed to be in that place for speech and mobility strengthening and training. As soon as I obtain the career I want my Momma will get the best care there is. I want her home to stay! My absolute favorite girl...I nicknamed her B.A.E.

Before
Anyone
Else

Nerdy pretty-eyed Dominique P. Thomas slipped up and got pregnant just after the start of the second year at Michigan State. Science major. Aunt Etta was making every attempt to be supportive, "It'll be ok Purp, I'll help you with the baby." I left college figuring I'd return when the baby got to be about six months old. That was not the case. I had twins, a boy and a girl. The sperm donor Pierre' was in and out of the picture. Of course, I thought that he and I were gonna be together forever as many young ladies think about their "man". Young and naive to say the least. As much as we were in "love" he sure started acting shitty after I told him I was pregnant.

Side-tracking and leaving college for a little longer than anticipated ''bout disappointed the fuck outta my ailin' Momma. I pushed through by the grace of God, Aunt Etta's support and my Ma of course. Earning my Masters in nursing was the end result. The kids and I moved approximately one hundred and fifty miles from where I grew up and although Aunt Etta didn't want to leave her place the invitation to come live with us is an open ended one...I respect and love her deeply.

Becoming a young mother of two (at once), returning to school, graduating working as a nurse consultant for a major law firm and buying a new home was a struggle in the beginning but well worth the awesome outcome. All great achievements at my age but at times I would feel like I hadn't "lived" boredom sank in. I started doing crazy and irresponsible shit. Being reckless as fuck. Partying with people from my old neighborhood. Drinking, licking, sucking, fucking, he, she, them. Being absolutely wild as hell.

I let the sperm donor keep the kids from time to time and that burned a hole in Aunt Etta's backside but she understood. She'd say, "All I know is my babies better not get hurt around his ass or he gone hafta deal with me and my posse." Momma said it gave Pierre's mom (Lynn aka Momma Lynn) an opportunity to get to know her grandbabies, which made sense. Momma was making great progress and just as I didn't have to want for anything, neither does she.

My ole punk assed daddy Cleveland Thomas, the well-known city whore and manipulating womanizer, wasn't even trynna get to know his grandbabies Demi and Denim. Trifling ass mothafuckuh. Maybe he's pissed because I went upside his head about my Momma. Oh well, I guess he will grow some brains one day, and if not, fuck 'em. Beat yo momma's ass, not mine!! He was always a low down scandalous mothafuckuh and got worse after my lil brother died. Ultimately, he would not let up. I was young but I remember a hell of a lot. I mean what the fuck? Donovan's death affected us all. Ok...let me stop...I'm gettin' teary.

A chick that I thought was a friend...known ole girl since childhood her name is Vicki. Ma never liked her and would say that she's jealous of me. But as we all know a hard head is recipe for a soft ass. Vicki is bisexual and can be a little on the aggressive side. Seems like she has always had a soft spot for me. While on a wild drinking and sexual binge she and I took a road trip to "The Windy City". We got bent. Totally shit face wasted. Ending up at the Ritz with some dude. We both fucked him. I have no idea what time it was but I woke to Vicki eating my pussy. Did I stop her? Nope...why not? I don't fuckin' know. It wasn't feelin' worth shit. For a second I thought the bitch was gonna try to eat me alive. If that broad would've bit me I was gonna whoop her ass. She didn't therefore I was like oh well and let her do her. She thought she was really puttin' it on me. I've never had to fake cumming, especially when gettin' my pussy ate. Damn. All I wanted to do was get the hell out of there and go home.

FOOD FOR THOUGHT...

Just because a bitch has a degree or three, a mega crib, a couple of vehicles and a fat income doesn't prevent her from being naughty or shall I say downright nasty. Prime example am I.

CHAPTER 1

A few years or around about following that total upset at the hotel Vicki catches me at a gas station. "Hey, hey lil sis!" I immediately thought huh? Lil sis? Naw bitch if I had a big sis she wouldn't be eating my cooch. Duh!! She says, "Girl, it's been a while but look I know this guy that'll be perfect for you, he's my man's friend." Oh, how is Charles? "No, Charles and I aren't together." "My new boo is Chris we've been seeing each other for about eight months." "Charles and I kept being 'on' and 'off' for the last year and a half." Oh, so your fass ass was fuckin' around on Charles with Chris and that's what the 'on' and 'off' again shit about. She giggled. I thought about it for a moment, a little reluctant and rightfully so but then I figured what the hell I may as well. I had been on chill mode for a while. All work and no play for the last couple years led my social/sex life in a downward spiral and I am in need of shaking that off. My babies and I are very close and although their love for me and mine for them is unconditional there's a void that I would not mind having filled. Therefore, I told Vicki to give the guy my number.

His name is Jordan, thirty years old with two children by different women. Why didn't it work out with either of those women? We text and talked for about 2 months sending video clips and pictures to one another. All those things do not measure up to seeing someone in person. He's handsome, intelligent, has a sense of humor and appears to be very gentleman-like.

This coming Friday at two o'clock in the afternoon…

THE MEET

While standing beside my purple Suburban sittin' on 26's I hear Anthony in the distance... "The Best of Me." Crisp air with the clouds cheerfully weaving their way in, on and around the sun I'd say it's about 72 degrees now and is supposed to reach 80 this spring day. Flaunting my beautiful dark brown-blonde tip oversized curls. Caramel skin fat face with deep dimples. Wearing a sky blue sleeveless silk blouse showing a lil cleavage and a navy blue above the knee skirt. Legs bare and as smooth as a baby's bottom with two inch heels that make me stand about five-foot ten. Weighing one hundred and seventy pounds curvy in all the right places. Every hardworking man or woman's dream.

I turn to the left nod slightly while fingering my D&G shades down to the bridge of my nose yes mothafucka notice these eyes. A fox and fine as hell so I've been told. A nerdy naughty educated hottie is what I know. Adjusting my shades fully back on and yes they're prescription I can't see shit without 'em. I glance up and see this tall 'bout six-foot three medium build dark skinned cutie. His hair is cut low/tapered. His eyes are brown and deeply mesmerizing, full lips and goutee'. A toss-up between Morris and Shemar. Weird? I know, right?!! But cute though.

He says, "Hey Miss Dominique I am thankful to be graced with your presence, it is my pleasure to meet you." (Oh my gosh his voice is even sexier in person). "I have enjoyed our texts and sweet but brief conversations. I am eager to learn more about you and of course Vicki has told me a little as well..." I hadn't seen her in a while and when I did she thought we'd be cool together in one form or another. We'll see now won't we? Everything else came from you which is a reliable source...correct? We laughed. "Yes", he replied. In regards to me you know the gist of it. I'm soon to be twenty-seven, I have six-year-old twins and very much independent. I don't have time for any games or bullshit we can be friends, associates I mean you seem pretty cool...let's hang out for a couple hours and take it from there.

(Clearing his throat)

"Straight-forward and understood." "Chris text me yesterday wanting to know if we could double date." "How about we let Vicki and Chris go their own way." "I can pay a sitter for the kids after we feed them and stuff of course." "Later you and I can catch a movie at the drive in. (With what sounded like fear in his voice) if you want." I informed him that Demi and Denim will be at my aunt's already...ok meet me back here in about 2 hours. "Will do Miss Dominique." I was gonna pull my SUV into the garage, instead with briefcase in hand I 'glam' walked it up to the house and yep he was lookin' and I was smilin'.

Can you say "Exhale."

I took a hot steamy shower, air dried and bunned my hair. Bali Mango body spray, peach, silver and dark blue basketball wives' earrings, Capri jeans and vest with a peach camisole underneath. Phoned Aunt Etta, "Just go ahead and enjoy yourself the twins are fine, we're going to the park and after that they'll bathe, eat and what not." "I've got it covered baby have fun I love you." I love you too Auntie.

Moments later the doorbell rings...it's Jordan

(yep I'm cheesin')

"I'm a few minutes early, didn't want you to cancel on me." I invited him in to have a seat in the living room. As I walked away he asked, "What is the fragrance you're wearing?" I replied so you work as a/an? Oh!! It's Bali Mango. "You wear it well, I manage two construction companies, one here and the other in Illinois." Cool I had forgotten if you owned them or...I'm sure it keeps you busy. As I told you I'm a nurse. "Yes, I bet it's challenging." Life's challenging Jordan. "Yeah it can be, I know all too well," he replied. I got my Louie bag and slid on the matching sandals. (Wow!! My mind is racing a million miles a minute, what am/was I thinking? I snapped at the guy...words to self, loosen up...breathe bitch breathe).

He smells so fuckin' good. Cream cotton shirt, khaki cargo shorts and black Nike's. His car is a silver Charger with factory rims. Shallow? Yes, I can be and hey roll with it or get rolled the fuck over. The choice is yours. He got the door for me saying, "This is a beautiful home you have." I looked up at him smiled and said thank you handsome, by the way you smell good as well. He chuckled as I got in the car. He then closed the door behind me. Chivalry may not be dead after all.

We arrived to Sharz. Valet gets my door and off we go. Sharz is a decent place well known for their succulent steaks and several unique appetizers. Speaking of 'em ours was a blooming onion which is a fried onion on steroids, grab a piece and dip it into your favorite sauce. I ordered a ribeye medium well, salad minus the tomatoes (yuck) a roll and iced tea. Jordan had tornado potatoes and a T-bone medium well with peach tea. Boy am I'm gonna pay for eating this. He asks, "How so?" "You're amazingly beautiful Dominique." I blushed.

After eating we snuck up on Aunt Etta and the kids at the park. My prince and princess bum-rushed me...oh how I love it!! "Hey babies! This is mommy's friend, Jordan." He squats and greets them. Denim stares at him while Demi says hi. They aren't used to seeing a man around their momma (with the exception of Bryce) and the sperm donor. He's living up to that term since he hasn't been parenting as he should. They are my heart and soul I love them with my everything.

Whose Bryce? Keep reading.

I introduced Jordan to Auntie. Then he, the kids and I began to walk towards an ice cream truck. Aunt Etta yells, "Dominique P. Thomas don't ruin my baby's appetites!" Hahaha yes sir sweet sticky old-fashioned vanilla ice cream cones. We played with the kids for a while. Jordan chased me. All I could do was run, laugh and scream at the same damn time. Aunt Etta giggled and looked on. That was exhilarating and well needed if I might add.

I received a call from the rehabilitation center Momma is in. Usually before the end of a long work week her case manager gives me a ring and at this time we are discussing discharge planning. "She's progressing quite well." I had noticed within the last two years that her speech and mobility is not one hundred percent but she's getting there. I will be moving her in and hire live-in assistance. Yep that's Bae. Jordan and I left the park. Now we're cruising and bumping some Kem. The evening was going great. We made it to the drive-in movie and to this day I cannot remember which movie we saw. Nonetheless the night ended perfectly. I was very pleased that Jordan did not make any sudden moves. Even though I had an enjoyable afternoon/evening it was a long one. Is this an actual gentleman? We shall see.

After getting in I took a long soak in my garden tub followed by air drying of course, while walking around the house in the buff as I usually do when I'm alone. Smiling and giving myself a pat on the back for being God fearing, attentive to my Ma and rearing my children the way I was taught. Very grateful to have had accomplished so much in so little time. I love my home. It's what I imagined having as a grownup. It's a little over fifty-two hundred square feet, the decor in the foyer is bright and modernistic with a couple of abstract paintings, there's five bedrooms, the master with private deck is on the main floor, the garden tub sits alone and the shower is eye catching, very large kitchen, living and dining areas, den, an office and bar. The second floor has four bedrooms, a full bath and a Jack and Jill, a library for the children and a play area, the basement is an unfurnished living area (with the exception of the area with a room and kitchenette) the rest is like another house with two bedrooms two and a half baths, full kitchen, along with a moderate sized theater space. The backyard has a deck that is half enclosed, a massive grilling station, jacuzzi and inground pool. My kitchen gives me the giggles...the overhead cookware hangin' above the granite island with double sinks is a bit different from how I grew up but Ma always talked of having such and now she does.

I donned a silk body wrap went to the bar off the living room and made me a drink called "Wet-Wet" which consists of vodka and frozen blended fruit with pineapple juice poured over crushed ice. I grabbed my laptop got comfy on the couch, checked my emails and there are a few people who have responded to the ad for live in help...cool! I hear my muffled cell (from my Louie bag). I jump up to get it hoping it was Jordan. It wasn't...it's Vicki. Cell phone in hand I plopped down on the sofa then noticed a text from Jordan and it read…

Hi beautiful! I enjoyed this evening and I would like to have the honor of continuing to see you. I hope to hear from you soon.

I grinned and text him back. I returned Vicki's call... she asked how did the date go of course. I gave her a lil info, thanked her and told her I was rather tired and I would fill her in on a later date. What Momma has said to me about Vicki I try to keep in mind. Although her being jealous of me is something I have failed to see. Even so I'm gonna stick with the notion... Momma knows best. Yes, I'm grown but I do try to listen and adhere to what my Mom says. I got up off the sofa double checked the house alarm, hit my playlist, grabbed my drink, sippin', singin' and off to bed I went.

Ahhhhh good night!

Rolled out of bed like a slinky this morning feeling damn good. I stepped out on my deck to take in some fresh air it's a little foggy out but I believe it's gonna be about 75 and sunny today. Back to my playlist and Sade it is. I took a shower then got dressed. White hoodie, yoga pants with a pink tank and Sketchers. Prior to picking my babies up I'll be stopping at a trail nearby. But beforehand I am notifying potential candidates for live in help via email to set up interviews.

Today, I'm rolling with my Challenger, it was given to me as incentive within my hiring contract... I have about a year or so remaining. En route listening to India Arie. Her music always makes for a nice drive. This trail is serene and the landscaping is beautiful. I'm glad it isn't flooding with people this morning. I put my Beats on and upped the tempo.

As I'm walking quite naturally I begin to think... I wouldn't trade my babies for all the tea in China and the feeling is mutual for Momma, I love her chunky ass. Aunt Etta is my girl. Now, this Jordan dude...I'd like to get to know and enjoy more of him. My options are open and I intend to leave it that way for a while. The career path I chose is rewarding in more ways than one. I am more of a paper nurse but initially I had to perform hands on care to gain experience. For instance, I've assisted surgeons in operating rooms but that is as close to "people" I'd normally get. My career skyrocketed at my current place of employment which is the:

Law Firm

of

Chandler, Danske and Rawls

I work with medical directors, chief surgeons and their attorneys in malpractice lawsuits. I analyze paperwork brought forth by insurance agencies. Major auto accidents, birth defects, surgical errors and so on. The pay is in no way shabby.

Three miles and done. I'm going back to the house to shower and change clothes. Durante jersey, jeans and Vans. I pulled my hair back into a ponytail then topped it with an OKC fitted. On the way to Aunt Etta's I listened to Pac "Ride on Our Enemies."

I arrive to Aunt Etta's and let myself in. I smell bacon and hear ole skool yep she is jammin'. Denim spots me, runs, jumps up and hugs me very tight. I whispered to him, "Hey Mommas baby," then I yelled, "Auntie it's smellin' good up in here!!" She peeps from the kitchen, "Heyy neicey Dominiqueee." I burst out laughing Auntie been sippin' and yep that's her. I grab a cup of grits and hooked up some blueberry waffles and we're jammin' right along. Aunt Etta tickles me. She's in here trying to B-bop. After the kids clean their toy room and eat, they're gonna wash up and then we're hitting the road. Aunt Etta hugs and kisses us all on our way out. "I may be by there sometime this week if not, the next...love yall." Ok Auntie we love you too. The kids and I stop by the mall and pick up a few spring outfits. They saw some schoolmates while there.

We get home and I prepare dinner which will be baked chicken wings, butter beans, brown rice and cornbread. My kids love some beans and cornbread, hell almost anything with cornbread. While I'm cooking the kids are playing in the backyard. I can see them from the kitchen, living room and dining area too. This open floor plan is structured to my liking. I'm gonna let the food do what it do while I take a look at some paperwork for a couple of cases that will be in court over the next few weeks. It's funny sometimes because people try to sue for the damnedest things...things that are usually their fault (such as failure to disclose an allergy to medication that they've known about all their life). It's the way of the world for some. I pick my cell up to text Jordan a hello and it rings. I almost dropped it...it's him.

"Hi how are you today?"

I'm fine Jordan, you?

(my palms all sweaty and shit)

"Me? Better now."

Aw that's sweet, are you working?

"Yes, I'm going to Illinois in about an hour...you?"

Being mommy and working from home.

"Nice. May I stop by before I leave…"

Sure.

"Great I'll be there in about 30 or so."

Mr. Construction man in the black F 150. I greet him and then we go out back. Demi smiles at him meanwhile Denim mean mugs him I believe. I thought uh-oh. It was cool seeing Jordan for a moment. He says he will probably be back in Michigan in about ten days or so, a couple weeks at the latest. I wished him a safe trip. As he was leaving out the door he turned to face me and slightly tugged at my chin, I closed my eyes, he planted his lips on mine, slid his tongue in my mouth…I'm suckin' on it and twirling my tongue with his. A wet and warm kiss that damn near left me breathless. The kids were snickering, we gave one another's hands a gentle squeeze and he left. Mmmumph!! I am smiling and looking downright goofy.

I look at the kids and ask what were yall laughing at? They took off running. I tackled and tickled them. They are too funny! We ate, they bathed, I read to them and then night-night.

These last few weeks of spring will be busy. Denim has karate class, cheering for Demi, I have them playing tennis as well. Yes, they're young and that's the time to motivate them and keep their minds stimulated. Extracurricular activities provide discipline as well. Keeping the body and mind at work. After all whatever the mind believes... the body can achieve. On another note, I am excited to have the interviews set up for the live- in help. I cannot wait until Momma comes home to us.

Out of the three interviews we have a winner, Ms. Cora. She won me over. God fearing, mature, experienced, professional, blunt and sassy. She reminds me of my Momma, Aunt Etta and my late maternal grandmother Ethel all wrapped into one. Never met anyone quite as forward as she is or can be. I believe I have that gene, that, God knows my heart but if ya fake you can kiss my entire ass. Yeah...that gene. It is what it is. Like my granny was Ms. Cora is...a fuckin' sweetheart. I offered her the job, she accepted. I then took her to meet Ma. Yes, I'm her momma now and if I'm happy with Ms. Cora Momma doesn't have a choice. (That's funny because 99.9999% of the time what she says goes).

Speaking of how people can remind you of someone, Demi reminds me of myself, exceptionally bright no glasses though. Denim is just like his deceased uncle Donovan, left-handed, kind hearted and hard headed. Ugh! Gettin' teary once again.

Jordan and I have been hit and/or miss for almost a month as far as seeing one another. Keeping in contact as much as our schedules will allow via texting, talking and video chatting. We have an upcoming dinner date at my house next Friday. Momma is progressing and I could not be happier for her. Ms. Cora has become very familiarized and she loves it here. There were subtle hints thrown at me that Aunt Etta wants to move in with us. My door is open for her...always.

THE MEET II

It's dinner date time! This should be interesting as all will be in attendance. Jordan arrived around four thirty and I'll be damned he looked even better. That turned me on. I greet him, introduce him to Momma and Ms. Cora. As I cooked he spoke with them and interacted with the twins. Jordan brought a little something which was nice. He brought Momma a single yellow rose, the kids a Dave and Busters gift card and as for me, a gift card as well his "secrets" are safe with me. He brought an after- dinner drink and to my surprise, some "marriage-ah-wanna." Dinner was fried pickerel (the kids had filet perch), salad and peas. Ms. Cora made carrot cupcakes. We ate, laughed. I helped Demi with bathing while the prince was in the den explaining a drawing to everyone. I finished up with my princess then told Denim to come on and bring it. Lookin' like I was in a wet T-shirt contest, nipples hard as hell, piercings exposed. I felt Jordan undressing me with those mesmerizing brown eyes. Blush-blush.

Ms. Cora was assisting Momma to her room to tidy up and get comfy. She is a great help and not only for Ma but the kids as well. I believe that kinda pissed Aunt Etta off. I would not be surprised if she was to show up at my door one day with all her things. Ms. Cora put the kids to bed. I changed into dry clothes, peeped in to check on Momma and she was asleep but not for long. I kissed her entire face.

Scrambled my way back to the kitchen and found Jordan loading the dishwasher. You didn't have to. "It's okay, Miss Dominique P. Thomas. I don't mind at all." He has me blushing once again. Bucket of ice and Grey Goose sitting on the island. That Grey!? Oh, hell that's my shit. I made us a drink then we tipped out onto the enclosed section of the deck (it's nippy out) to smoke some weed. On the way back into the house Jordan asks…" So, what does the P stand for?" Pussy. (I cannot believe I said that with a straight face). Laughing I followed with, you don't want to know. The weed had me giggly as hell. I hadn't smoked any in about four years and yes, this will be the last time. Grey had me feeling all warm and tingly. I wasn't mad at all, just enjoying the moment.

I said take three guesses. He says, "Patricia." Nope. "Hmmm Paulette?" Way off. "Let me see…Penny?" Funny you should say that because I randomly say penny and at that moment I want to know what the person is thinking but no. It's Purple. He laughed and said, "You've gotta be kidding." No, I'm not. We both giggled. "Why, do you know why your Ma chose Purple?" Yes, I do, It's the color of my birthmark. As he sat on the sofa he says,"Let me see it." Soon Jordan…very,

very soon. I put a DVD on of stand-up comedy then joined him on the sofa. Five different comedians. They had our sides splittin'!

Jordan refreshed our drinks. We talked about his children both who live in Illinois. Two girls, Takiss, nine and Shayla, eleven. He has a younger brother Travis, who is a junior at my alma mater. Jordan doesn't know his biological father. Travis' dad ran off as well. His mother is no longer living and he didn't wish to discuss it. I can respect that.

We talked and sipped. Just as I was about to ask if he wanted to listen to some music he took my drink, sat 'em both on the solid space on the ottoman then he stood in front of me taking my hand. I felt kind of nervous my palms were beginning to sweat. He kissed my neck, ears then my neck again. I felt weak. My pussy started throbbing. Yes! He placed his left hand behind my head, his right one on my cheek, bringing me closer to him. I closed my eyes, he licked my lips then started suckin' and kissin 'em I was doing the same in return. My hands are under his shirt rubbing from his back to his sides. He tugged my hair a little, my head went back, he then devoured my neck and shoulders while loosening my bra. Grabbing me closer he lies me on the sofa then he starts to tongue my covered bra-less hard assed pierced nipples.

Using his teeth, he began to pull my blouse up inch by inch. Licking my navel. I started moaning.

I began to squirm in anticipation as to what'd be next. He came up and passionately tongue kissed the shit outta me. I was seein' stars, glittered rainbows and shit. Thinkin' he's gonna fuck my brains out!!

I kissed his cheeks and ears nibbling away, while his hands roamed down between my thighs caressing my pussy (outside of my clothes) I'm hotter than a mothafucka. I grabbed his hand and whispered his name. He kisses me and said, "yes." Come...let's go to my room (which is on the other side of the house). I tapped him...you're it!! Then, I jumped up and took off running so did he. I lit candles, turned some jazz on then I began to undress and he said… "No, let me."

He turned me around (my back to him) lifts my blouse and removes it. Hugging me from behind his bare chest against me. Ahhh. Oh my, this felt like...hmmm I can't even begin to explain it. Damn he smells so fucking good. He unbuttoned, unzipped my pants pulled them down some. He gave my back a wet and warm tongue thrashing. I was trembling. Then in amazement he says, "Oh here it is!" I chuckled, my purple birthmark is just above my left butt-cheek. He sat on the end of my California King. While kissing my birthmark he pulled my pants all the way down and off.

Standing there stark naked he turns me around kisses my pussy (pubic area) then he slides his tongue between my lips. Oh fuck! I almost lost my balance but nope, he had me by the hips. Hell, I thought I was gonna faint. As he moves backward (onto the bed) he pulls me along. I'm straddling him, licking, sucking and blowing on those ears he moans and mumbles my name while his hand caresses my wet pussy. I reach back and feel his rock hard assed dick. (I figure about nine inches...hmmm maybe ten). I whisper hold up. "Oh, I got you," he replied. He reaches for his pants and takes two condoms from his wallet. "Come here you," he says while pulling me closer by my sides positioning me to straddle his face. He started kissing my thighs (oh the anticipation) parted my lips with his tongue then began to thrust my vagina with it, licking and sucking on my clit as I rode his face (got-damn tongue moving like a bullet). I'm moaning loudly. Jor, Jor, Jordaaaan. I screech and started quakin' he grabbed my ass cheeks and wouldn't let go...kept lickin' and suckin' my clit. I came all over his face screamin' GoTdAmNit!!

Reaching back caressing that big thick dick, he lifts me up and guides me onto it...slowly, slowly. He started moaning. I was mumbling ahh ok, ok ahh. My wetness allowed my walls to become one with his thickness, I started riding that dick. He was handling the fuck outta me. Then lifting me up and closer to him he kisses me. Pullin' my hair, lickin' and suckin' the front side of my upper body. He lies me down then we began to hurriedly and sloppily kiss. He's on top of me. Legs wide open I want him deep, deep inside. Easing his dick inside of me I moan. He moans as he goes a lil deeper. My heels on them shoulders...damn he's puttin' his back into it. Whispering my name followed by whispers of, "Oh, ooh shit I'm...uhhh...ahh." He grabs me, the sheets and the stroke is long and the grind is deep. I'm cradling his head. He's having aftershocks of a nut out of this world. Our bodies are moist. As we held each other we kissed and he dozed off. I laid there for a few minutes thinkin'...wow! I've been missing shit like this? With that being thought, good night.

Awakened by my blaring alarm. (I forgot to deactivate it). It's Saturday morning...seven to be exact. Jordan is snugged all under me. I reach to turn the alarm off he tugs at my side. "Good morning beautiful." I smiled lookin' like Miss Celie. "Good morning," I replied. He kisses my nose and lips. Moments later we were kissing and caressing one another while showering. We exit. Would you like some coffee? "Yes, I'd love a cup before I leave." I ski-dattled to the kitchen giggling inside which matched the goofy grin on my face. The entire house was quiet with-the-exception of Ms. Cora, she was gathering laundry and had coffee brewing.

Jordan was lying there with his boxers on, sat up took the coffee and said, "Thank you." Then he kissed the back of my hand. I winked and replied, you're welcome. "What's on your agenda for today?" For starters, I'm stealing my Aunt Etta away from whatever she's doing and having brunch with her. Until then wake everyone up and watch cartoons. You said something about going to Illinois today for about four to six hours correct? "Yes, you guys are more than welcome to come." What time? "It can be anytime I have to check servicing on some equipment." We'll see and if not today another time. Either way I'll keep you posted.

"Ok Miss Dominique." He picked me up...straight up. I chuckled. We kissed. He sat me down on the end of the bed, got dressed and then I saw him out.

CHAPTER 2

During Momma's illness and recovery period she had not given up her spunk nor her sense of humor. She has kept me in good spirits through many trials despite her woes. She's heaven sent. At one point, she spoke to me about not wanting to be a burden. Well I guess I'm gonna have to tie you down and spank yo' juicy butt because you're not going anywhere Mom Dukes. She laughed 'til her sides hurt and chuckled, "Don't whoop me momma." The look on her face when she said that was priceless. Never a burden, always my Mother.

This morning she's at it. "So, you like this Jordan huh, how old is he, he told me he has two daughters, has he ever been married, he told me he manages a couple of companies or something, what does he have to offer...?" She started sniffing me as I was hugging her. "Mmhmm I know what you were doing." I replied, huh? "I smell a stench of cologne on you. We both fell out laughing. "Where's Bryce, thought I forgot about him, is he, did he...?" Momma you are too much (I said while giggling and stammering). Then of course... "Jordan's girls aren't too far apart in age, are they by the same woman or does he have two baby mommas...if so what happened that neither of those worked out?" I didn't know and my intent is to enjoy him while we're "messin" it ain't like

I'm trynna marry his ass. Those were my thoughts (didn't say that shit out loud) I wouldn't dare curse around Momma. I kissed her forehead and said we will talk later she looked at me like...what you thought? We weren't?

The chaps and I ate Jethro Bodine bowls of cereal while Ms. Cora made egg white omelette's for Momma and herself. Now we're all watching cartoons in the theater room or shall I say the cartoons are watching us. Meanwhile the kids and I are tickling the buh-jee-beez out of each other. Momma's on her blue-tooth talking to Auntie. "Baby Purp (uggh that's the nickname Ma gave me) my sister is on the way over." Cool! Aye Momma tell her I was gonna steal her away for a little while today. Let her know that I will come and get her. "She said for a while, un huh... she'll see you shortly." The kids yelled "Ooouuuu Ma you in trouble!" I tackle, tickle and kiss 'em they both "broke" away and took off runnin'.

After picking Aunt Etta up she and I ate at Golden Corral. Afterward we stopped by the gym and yes, she asked damn near the same questions Momma had asked about Jordan. I'm like wow! Ok... I like him and stuff. She says, "You're smiling way more than usual and the way you walking..." Huh? "More like you switching lil lady." Whew! (I thought the shocks from that dick was...). Hahaha Auntie you trippin' "Yeah whatever, trippin' my eye." We laughed. We showered at the gym.

Got back to the house and Aunt Etta joined Momma, Ms. Cora and one of Ma's long-time friends Ms. Rose. Our neighbor Mrs. Johnston has two little boys and custody of her little niece whose six years old. She invited the kids for a play date. They'll be gone for about three hours or so.

I made me a Wet-Wet then went into my office to edit some files for an upcoming case involving one of Michigan's finest medical directors. After the editing is completed I will submit the file to one of the corporate attorneys.

I text Jordan…

> Hey you! I hope all is going well at the site.
> I'm doin' a lil work from home right now, the kids are on a play date.
> Sorry I didn't get back to you earlier.
> TTYS

He immediately returned a text:

> Miss Dominique, hello beautiful. Yes, all is well.
> Wish I didn't have to leave today but I will
> See you soon ;-)

Smiling, I sent him a wink face back. I keep having flashbacks about last night. My pussy jumpin' and achy in a good way. Ok I'm almost finished submitting this work and when it's completed mani/pedi here I come.

Momma and company left to go play bingo. While getting my pedicure I get a call from Ms. Johnston she's feeding the children and they will probably go to a movie. Jordan and I talked a little about how our day is going. He seems to like me. I'm not sure if it's like or lust that I feel. Hell, I hadn't been sexed like that in forever. Gonna play it by ear and see how it goes. (Mani/pedi done).

Before I head back to the house I will grab me a bite to eat but right now I'm gonna shop a little. I want some accessories among a few other things. There's an outlet nearby, I'm about to be like a kid in a candy store!

First, the Nike outlet. Yes! Memory foam sandals for everyone. Hmmm I figure Ms. Cora to be about a size eight. I'm getting a salmon color, my prince brown, my princess fuchsia, purple for Momma and Aunt Etta...red for Ms. Cora. I'm sure everyone will like them. They're absolutely comfortable. Gonna snatch up a couple pair of sneakers for the gym/walking. I've gotta get the twins some too. Next stop...Perfume Mania.

THE PAST

While testing some Donna someone touches my left shoulder, "Dominique?" I turn and oh my goodness it's this chick I used to mess around with during (my senior year@ MSU) and right after college. We lost contact or should I say I lost contact. I wasn't sure if a "lesbian" lifestyle is what I wanted. Oh wow! Hey Sam (Samantha)! How have you been? "I've been fine Dominique although I've been better, you're absolutely beautiful." (Damn woman has me blushin') Thank you Sam. You're looking and smelling good as always. "Can we grab a cup of coffee and chat for a minute?" Sure, let me pay for this and we can go over to Starbucks. She took my bags. Still the gentlewoman I see. "Yes, that hasn't changed." As she smiles and tries to cover up blushing she asks, "So how's work?" I told her for whom I work for and details.

So, Sam did you take your dad up on his offer? "He passed and I wouldn't have felt right if I hadn't taken over the business." Oh, Samantha I am so very, very sorry (as I hugged her tightly). What happened if you don't mind me asking. "Of course not, not at all." "He passed on in his sleep out of nowhere...just like that." "I'm grateful it wasn't a situation whereas he suffered for months, years." Exactly. Damn baby I am so sorry that really hurts...gotdamnit have mercy. She placed her order. Then I. Let me have a venti soy caramel macchiato with an extra shot of expresso and three raw sugars upside down. We got our drinks...walked over to a table she pulls my chair out of course. We sit and chat.

Kissing the back of my hand oh so very gently. She misses me. I've missed her too. We dated for over a year. The love and comfort of a woman is amazing but I don't think I want to live that life...I don't know. We exchanged numbers, emails and physical addresses. I'm gonna hit the Levi outlet, that's where Sam had come from just beforehand. She asked to tag along with me.

Sam's five foot eleven, dark skinned, naturally thick lashes, she has the prettiest white straight teeth and a smile that's melting, one deep dimple to the left cheek, lengthy, beautiful healthy locs, athletic build, tits about a b-cup. She always smells good, cologne not too heavy and stays dressed GQ she is so boyish...I LOVE that! Nothing like a girl being a boi. Sam is a no filter kinda fine. I purchased a few things from Levi. She walks me to my SUV, puts the bags on the back seat, gets my door, kisses my forehead then grabs and kisses the back of my hand. "Be sure to call me Dominique." I will Sam, I will. While driving back home nibbling on a panini this woman has me thinking about what we used to have. I was happy but afraid I guess.

Overall it was a great weekend. Everyone got a little air and enjoyed their personal space. They all liked their sandals. In about ten days school will be out for the summer and my babies will be going to camp (two over the summer). They finally like it, the first couple times was a trip. Ms. Cora will accompany Momma on her appointments. When I am not required to be in the office I will accompany her myself.

Every aspect of my life is on cruise control…

Next school year Demi will be playing the flute. Denim is just like his uncle he loves football and so do I. Momma trying to get sassy. Her clothing, makeup and lil accessories. I'm loving it. We're blessed she has come a long way. Last we heard, my dad may have been killed in Jersey. We're not for certain. I wasn't gonna lose any sleep over it and neither was Ma. She's grateful he didn't kill her and so am I because I'd be without a Mother and definitely without a father because I would have killed him.

REACQUAINTING

While at the office I received an email...

The aforementioned Bryce. Bryce Chandler hence the law firm of Chandler, Danske and Rawls. He's a partner that has hit on me off and on for quite some time but he was married. Even though he'd say his marriage was "rocky", I do not involve myself with married men. Now that he's divorced he's trynna holla once again. Says he's been praying that I'm still single. Meet and sleep with Jordan and here comes Bryce's ass. Hey, he's fair game and so am I. He knows a great deal about me and I of him. He would keep me laughing and smiling at corporate retreats, luncheons and depositions. He has met my children on a few occasions like corporate picnics and family oriented company outings. His then wife never accompanied him.

Bryce is thirty- one- years old, about six-foot five, fit, jet black hair, seductive blue eyes and perfect teeth. Yes, he's caucasian and scrumptious. He smells fantabulous all the time. He attended Morehouse, the male "Black" college. His passion for basketball landed him there not to mention his wits (several scholarships). He received financial help from his family of course but he worked while in school just to have and maintain a sense of independence. The firm was established by his great grandfather. The wealth of his family did not make him a brat. Bryce was gonna initiate a firm of his own, instead he continued his family's legacy which was a smart idea.

His ex-wife Lisa, a wanna be bourgeoise black woman. They met during their college years, she attended Georgia State University. She left school when they got married. He says that she had no desire to have children and Bryce had an issue with that. It hurt him badly. He couldn't understand why she hadn't mentioned it during their courtship, engagement or honeymoon even. In his eye's he saw her as selfish. He asked for my opinion a while back and I told him...Lisa appears to be the gold digging type and hey it is what it is. I truly believe deep down he figured the same thing. They had an itemized prenuptial agreement. I hope he had given her a decent settlement though. After all she married him.

As I was emailing him back an intern knocks and enters my office with probably three/four dozen multicolored roses on a cart. I am immediately drawn to them and began sniffing them like mad. The card read:

The Special Occasion Is…
YOU
Xoxoxoxoxoxo BRYCE

I'm smiling from ear to ear and beetly blushing. An email comes to me... "Ok you can stop smiling now...nah go ahead." "I yearn to hold you and I can't wait." "How's the prince and princess, your mom...aunt?" -----A lot has been going on we'll catch up very soon. I can't wait either. Talk to you later...xoxoxoxo

A day of work completed and it wasn't a hard one. As I pulled into the driveway I notice Ms. Cora doodling about in the yard. She approaches me as I'm getting out of the car and takes the roses. I grab my purse and briefcase. Took my shoes off at the door and proceeded toward my bedroom en route I sat my briefcase in my office. Ma was taking a nap. I took a quick shower, grabbed my cell, went to the living room and got comfy on the couch...chillin' waiting on my babies to get home. They should be here in about an hour. Meanwhile Ms. Cora is preparing dinner.

I get a call from Vicki, "What's up chick, how are you and Jordan doing?" Girl I'm fine, chillaxin' waiting on my little ones to get home. We kick it and keep in touch. "Oh... ok y'all think y'all wanna double date soon?" I guess...hell I don't know but I'll hit you up. Uggh girl bye! Bitch didn't ask how my kids or Momma doing. Shit Momma is about right, that heifer doesn't like me and probably is jealous. Anyhow she can kiss miss me with that bullshit.

CHAPTER 3

For some reason Sam runs across my mind. Damn. I don't know if that's a good idea. I surely do not want her to think that she's being led on. I can truly say that I miss her as a lover and a friend. Let me give her a call. "Hello Dominique." Hiya Sam what you up to? "I'm about to leave the clinic shortly." Oh, I apologize, didn't know you were working. "No apology needed, I'd move mountains for you Dominique." "I love you still and always will." I love you too. I just wanted to tell you that I miss you. I'm not trying to rekindle our relationship I want you in my life as my friend. I don't know if you'd be willing. It may be hard for me at first but I'm sure, "Yes of course I'm willing to try." Maybe we could meet sometime soon. Until then we can text and talk as well. I ended the call to let her finish working… gotta take care of the pets!

It's warm so I went out onto the back deck and not even five minutes later Ms. Cora peeps out…

"Miss Dominique, Jordan is here." I thought wow! Really? Unexpectedly? Somebody better tell his ass. I get up to enter the house and in doing so he's smack dab in front of me attempting to kiss me. I gave him a peck. "What's wrong," he asks. I kindly let him know that I'd appreciate it if he'd never, ever come to home unexpectedly. No call, no text...I don't play that shit. He pleaded for my forgiveness and stated he'd never do it again. "I missed you so much Dominique." I allowed him to join me on the deck. We began to talk about his work, there's an upcoming outing the construction company is gonna sponsor at Nedayah water park (all the while I'm texting Bryce). I agree to go to the outing. Just then the kids arrive. Bryce is aware of Jordan. He doesn't like it but he doesn't care he wants me.

Denim and Demi bombard me with their lil sweaty bodies and they spoke to Jordan. I asked him if he liked to join us for dinner-he did. After dinner the kids, Jordan, Momma, Ms. Cora and I played this video game, something like the feud. It was fun. Later that night, Bryce and I talked for hours. We made plans to spend some time together very soon.

I took this afternoon off to accompany Momma to a doctor's appointment. She was walking faster than me...you go Ma! I suggested a pedicure and massage for Ms. Cora, on me, of course. Momma and I had a late lunch and chatted a bit. A little about my brother. She wanted to know how was I feeling and if I was ok behind his death. "I know it has been years but I remember it like it was yesterday." I bet so Momma he was your baby. We both became teary. Hugged.

Then she started in on Bryce. "What's going on young lady? You've got a glow...is Bryce in your life now? Did he get his long-awaited divorce?" Sort of and yes. "What do you mean sort of? Either he's in our...I mean your life or not (chucklin')." We've been talking and texting. I bump into him at work from time to time as well. "Baby Purp, I know you've been liking him for a while, soooo..." Momma! Stop (laughing) we'll see, you'll be the third person to know. "And Jordan?" Ma...I, "Look baby, I can't put my finger on it but there's something about him. Please be careful Baby Purp. People are and can be crazy." I will Momma. She grabbed my wrist tightly, "Please, please I know you're grown baby and I could very well be wrong but nonetheless we have to very mindful of THE COMPANY WE KEEP." She kissed my hand, hugged me very tight then planted one on my forehead, nose, cheeks and pecked my lips.

School will be out for the summer next Thursday and the following Thursday my babies will leave for camp Nature Ale for three weeks then back home for one week before going off to tennis camp. I miss them when they're not here but they will be learning a lot. Discipline for one which is a requirement for balance at home, school, socially and so on. Meanwhile there is no school this coming Thursday or Friday therefore the prince and princess will be spending this long weekend at their grandma's. Momma Lynn (Pierre's mother) will pick them up from school on Wednesday and I will get them from her place on Sunday, that's if she doesn't decide to bring them home. I dropped Ma off at Aunt Etta's, she's gonna be over there for a few days. When I got back home I took about an hour soak in my garden tub and now I'm on my private deck reading one of my all-time favorites... Luckily Seasons Change. I love it.

It's the end of hump/work day. Jordan text me a couple times as I was working earlier today, I could've returned them but I didn't. I don't know if he's starting to bore me or if it's what Momma said. She has never steered me wrong. Not purposely. I mean the sex was good but I think I better take heed.

I spoke with Sam this morning and she'd like to hangout this weekend...will do. Her idea of hanging out is paintball or Dave's. I enjoy it and her as well. I packed a couple of bags because she is just as spontaneous as I am. Bryce is away on business and although he wanted me to go with him, I had to see my babies beforehand. I could catch a flight but I don't wanna chill while he works. I'd probably shop like mad. I know he wouldn't mind but I'd like to have another kind of fun.

I had a blast with Sam over the weekend and yes paintball it was. Silly goose kept trying to shoot my butt and she didn't miss many times. She had my right ass cheek sore and made many promises to kiss it and make it better. Following paint-ball we stopped by her place and took quick showers. As I was air drying in her den area she yelled for me to bring her the blow-dryer from the bathroom where I had taken my shower. As I entered her bedroom she was drying off with a towel and yes, I was glancing at those perky tits and nicely svelte body.

While drooling I imagined...handing her the blow-dryer, she lightly tugs at my arm pulling me closer and slides her tongue in my mouth then two fingers in my pussy as we sloppily yet passionately kiss while she fingers the fuck outta me. Immediately I snap out of it, slurp the drool away and hand her the blow-dryer. As I walked away I said, still looking good in the buff. There was no need for me to look back I knew she was blushing.

We got dressed and went to Marcianos...an Italian restaurant. She talked about her nieces and two women that she has tried to pursue but had no luck. I told her it's their loss. There is a young lady that she has an eye on though. Her name is Tiffani. I hope she takes interest in you, you're a magnificent woman. Ever wanna talk I'm here. I told her about my situation and she says, "Listen to your Ma Purp...please." While dropping me off at home she says, "I'm here for you at absolutely any given time you just remember that." After settling at our humble abodes part of the night we texted about sports. It was cool. During and for the rest of the night Bryce and I video chatted.

DEVASTATION

Bryce and I had lunch now we're sipping on coffee awaiting his driver. While doing so I received a call from Ms. Cora. "Dominique... Miss Dominique I have disturbing news (my heart dropped), Pierre's mother said she couldn't reach you so she called the house and he has been shot and it is not looking too good. Having a stunned expression Bryce takes my cell, grabs and holds me close and begins to talk with Ms. Cora. "Yes ma'am I do...ok no problem I will take care of her." As he held me I became limp. "Oh, baby I am so sorry, I'm gonna get you to the hospital right away." His driver arrives and Bryce does everything aside of carry me. I was trying my best to hold my composure.

The twins' dad (good ole sperm donor) had been shot. I do not hate Pierre' by no means, hell I have a love for him and was in love with him at one point with his slick talkin' fine ass. I hope that he isn't too badly wounded. If that's the case I pray he doesn't suffer. If he pulls through I'm gonna kick 'em in the butt.

Arm in arm with Bryce we arrive to the hospital's ED. I see Momma Lynn pacing in the trauma waiting area she looks up at me with bloodshot eyes and her arms open wide.

I went running to her she started crying and screaming out, "My baby Nique!" "Somebody killed my baby!!" Bryce was on my heels knowing I was gonna need him. I reach her, we hug, cry, yell and squeeze each other so fuckin' tight. Bawlin' our eyes out. Tears streamed down Bryce's face. He knew a great deal about the prince and princesses' dad.

We didn't stay at the hospital too long. Pierre's family is small and the majority of them live in California. I offered Momma Lynn to stay over at my house, she really doesn't have anyone here in Michigan other than a drug addicted brother, a niece whose incarcerated and her baby Pierre of course. She agreed to stay and I'm glad about that...I did not want her to be alone.

Momma Lynn was told that Pierre was coming out of a gas station and was shot. Not robbed or anything. Just shot for no apparent reason. There were cameras present, an investigation is underway. Bryce hadn't left my side and I didn't want him to. Ma and Aunt Etta are in shock. Ms. Cora is very sweet and consoling to everyone. I text Sam, she was in disbelief as well and offered to come by. I told her maybe in a day or so because I am truly drained. I'll tell the twins when we pick them up from camp in at least a day or two.

Jesus that was a very rocky night to get through but we managed. So many fucking unanswered questions is all… and the main one being…WHY?!??

The following day we discussed funeral arrangements. Bryce left only for a moment to go to a nearby department store for a few changes of clothes. Otherwise he remained present. My damn phone was blowing up…Vicki and other people from my old neighborhood. I'll get back to them when I can. Now that we have the funeral arrangements completed and the house is calm I was gonna order take-out but Ms. Cora insisted on cooking. We all ate a lil bit.

The next day Bryce's driver took us to get my babies. We explained that Papi is gone and not coming back. They understood but wanted to know the how's and why's. Before getting back into the SUV all Momma Lynn could do was get teary and hold them very close. Bryce and I tried to explain to the children to the best of our ability. As we were riding along Demi was snug under Bryce and Denim under me.

DEPARTURE

The funeral service was very nice. Mm, mm, mm Pierre'. It broke me down to see him just lying there...his fine Latina ass. His favorite color was brown therefore brown, beige and a burnt orange color is what he wore and so did we. I put the kid's favorite colors in the center of his casket spray. Yellow, fuschia and blue carnations centered many burnt orange, brown and beige colored roses.

Memories were stormin' my mind.... we'd laugh, argue, makeup, make out, eat, shop and do it all over again. As I once said...he started acting shitty when I told him I was pregnant but that changed thanks to Momma Lynn. My heart aches for her, my babies, Ma and myself as well but Pierre' knows no more pain, worrying or suffering...he's done what we all must. Even so, I despise it having to be this way. Tragic. The unknowns. Hell Pierre' wasn't about that life-the streets/hood violence/drugs.

My Ma is so hurt that was her grandbabies' daddy, she and Momma Lynn comforted one another. Son/son in law type of deal, damn...gotdamnit! I pray the authorities find a person of interest, suspect, murderer. My heads spinning and what better place to rest it other than on Bryce's chest. I feel so safe when he's in my presence. I find comfort and peace with him.

There was a gathering at Local 212 following the funeral service. Vicki had come and was acting sort of strange, I mean she hugged us all but something felt weird or it could just be this sudden loss that has me feeling this way. She asked me where's Jordan... I side-eyed this bitch so viciously. "Not here obviously," Bryce stated. She walked away. This man is by my side the entire time supporting me and my family and you have the audacity to ask me where the fuck is Jordan? Bitch please. I certainly texted him to let him know what happened and his response was a dry one therefore I let it be. My kid's dad has just been killed I do not have time for games or people being wrapped up in their feelings. I can't drizzle a fuck right now.

Sam had come to show her respect. She spoke with Bryce and told him if there's anything that she can do, do not hesitate and she gave him her card. I was having a lil drink and trying to relax. Sam turns to me and that hug was none other than genuine/heartfelt. She then pecked my forehead, nose and then my cheeks. "I love you all and always will, I am very, very sorry for your loss Purp." Ma and Aunt Etta nodded and slightly rolled their eyes at her, they knew she and I had been together and wasn't fond of her but I made my choices. They need to let it go.

Momma Lynn had Pierre' cremated. She told me that she could not bear the thought of putting and leaving him in the ground. The urn was beautiful. She offered me ashes and of course I accepted them. I had some of the cremains placed in necklaces to be given to the kids when they're older. I had my portion of the cremains put into this white gold frame and placed a picture of Pierre' holding the twins in it. Momma Lynn didn't want to live in her place so I got movers to put her things in storage while we looked for another place. Aunt Etta was extremely helpful with everything. I praise Ms. Cora for her efforts she's amazing as well.

MOVING RIGHT ALONG...

The following month Momma Lynn had a very spacious three-bedroom apartment. Bryce was glued to my ass even when he wasn't present...I love it. Although he has people employed to do several things I wanted him to go and check on his penthouse. He gave me this puppy dog face that about broke my heart. I just wanted everyone to try to get themselves together. We will grieve, laugh and get past this one day at a time.

DISGUST and DESPAIR

I have umpteen texts from Jordan and while going through them he calls me. We talked for about thirty minutes or so. He wanted to come by or meet me. I chose the latter. We met at Sadie's Soul Food. He looked stressed and it appeared as if he lost a couple pounds. The topic of discussion (for him) was not seeing or being able to see one another. Meanwhile I was more concerned about Pierre's death...funeral and no hear from. He said, "The corporation of the construction companies I manage took a downfall. I was receiving subliminal threats. I had been overwhelmed." Threats? Why...what the? "I apologize from the bottom of my heart for not being there during your time of need." Yeah that was fucked up but it's all good. I have God, my family and Bryce who's a great guy. I commend him for staying by my side. "Yeah I know." Really?!! How so? Ya know what fuck it. Being extremely heated from his response I hadn't realized a missed call from Bryce.

I gathered myself, headed to my car and called him. I sounded upset he asked me what was wrong, I told him it's just a temporary matter. "About?" That guy Jordan. He wanted to apologize face to face for not being there during my time of need. He was rambling on about being threatened about something or another I don't know. "Umph what the hell, he…" I told him apology accepted. "So, what made my lady upset?" (I blushed) He asked about you or should I say it was the sarcasm in his voice. I'm sure Vicki is how he knows of you. Either way I can't understand why he would converse with her and not reach out to me for a simple condolence. Sighing. I'm about to be… (there's a knock on the car window scaring the shit outta me). What the… it's Jordan. (I barely open the window).

What's up Jordan?

(Bryce sighs in my ear)

"I'm sorry Dominique please don't be this way, I'm having a rough time, even so I had fallen for…"

Bryce: Baby leave! He'll be fine. I do not trust him and I want you safe.

I let the window up as I drove off waving bye. I placed the phone on the car's blue-tooth and hit the road. Bryce told me that he'd be to my house in a few of hours and not to worry about anything…bills/money and to return to work when I feel up to it. I expressed my appreciation and thanked him for his thoughtfulness as well. I'm gonna work from home for a couple of weeks that way I can spend some time with my babies before school starts again. I'm pulling into my driveway and telling Bryce that I'm turning my cell off and to call the house phone if he needs to reach me before getting here.

The kids will be home in a couple of days. I called to check on them and their camp leader expressed, "They're just fine, no concerns, no worries at this time." After that call, I went to lay my head across my Ma's chest. She rubbed and kissed my forehead repeatedly. I told her of the incident and very sternly she said, "Steer clear of that mothaf..." I will Momma.

CHAPTER 4

Bryce and I showered then got in bed. He knew Jordan had really gotten under my skin therefore he caressed my body in its entirety (from my hair follicles to my toenails). Releasing tension with every touch. My woes… there wasn't any. Lying there with my limbs spread I didn't have a care in the world.

Meanwhile my nipples are rock hard and tingling with anticipation… just then his warm mouth became one with my breasts and his tongue twirled on my nipples tantalizing my entire being. He (I'm moaning) gently cuffs then uncuffs my pussy repeatedly and with each cuff his grip gets stronger. Then he parts my lips with his fingers and slides two of them inside my wet throbbing pussy. I began to gently grind. I was feeling flushed ya know like my insides were crying tears of joy that it longed for. That firm manhood of his presses against my thigh and as he's feasting on these perky double D's I gently massage his head then firmly grasping him by the hair pulling him to my mouth and we kissed. A kiss like none I've ever felt before, not only do I feel ecstasy beyond my wildest dreams…I FEEL LOVE!!

Before I knew it, we were out of bed and he had me against the wall fervently kissing and biting my breasts, belly and sides...I am lightly tugging at his hair and massaging his scalp we're both moaning. Those strong hands grasp my thighs opens them and.... ahhh he tastes me!! My clit is so fuckin hard I'm so wet. Mmmmm, ooouuu my knees weaken...he takes control and grabs the back of my thighs lifts me up and kisses away any doubts/fears all while guiding himself inside of me. Gotdamn! This dick though. Thick as fuck and filling my canal tightly. With each thrust and grind we moan simultaneously. He's so e-v-e-r-y thing. Tightening his grip on my hips and ass. I grind. As I'm squirting he says, "Uhhh fuck." He moans loudly "Ahh shhhhit..." We came in unison. He carried me over to the bed while remaining inside of me. We felt one another throbbing and the sensation was damn good! We lie in bed tightly holding each other and captivated in one another. We fell asleep.

I wake to Bryce looking at me, smiling and saying, "You're gorgeous without effort, I could watch you sleep anytime." (he moves even closer to me) "Oh yeah let me see..." I asked what are you... "Yes, your morning breath, I thought I liked it before but to actually ..." You're silly baby. Well since you like my morn...he kisses me, my breasts then one finger, two, three...I squirm upward a little; he firmly grasps my hip with the other hand as he passionately and slowly fills me with those three fingers. Just then he takes them out and devours them. Meanwhile he plants a wet one on me and adds a finger to the kiss...mmmm yes to taste the essence of me from his finger(s) was exhilarating. Kissing, nibbling, biting him ahhh shit yeah. His thickness enters my impatiently waiting moist box...ah, mmhmm, uhh, ahhh, Bryce...he withdraws and immediately insert those three fingers. I grind. He covers my clit with that warm wet mouth of his and oh God...ohhh that tongue rotation!!! I came twice and begged him to stop. "No." He flipped me over bit my ass cheeks and tore my pussy up from the back...oh my, my, my, my...FUCK!! Say what you want about white boys. This brother has it together thank you, ex-wife of his. Next time we're gonna utilize my cuffs and silk scarves.

We took a long hot and steamy shower discussing our upcoming hookie time which will take place in a couple weeks. I made us breakfast toasted bagels, eggs over easy, bacon, grits and coffee. I took it to my private deck and as I handed him the coffee he sat it down and says, "I love you Dominique. I love Demi, Denim and your mother." "I'm sure this comes as no surprise."

"Not only do I love you I am in love with you." I have loved you for quite some time Bryce and I fell in love with you somewhere during that time. We stood there holding each other and became emotional. After we ate he got ready for a flight to catch to Los Angeles. He wanted me to go and so did I but I will be busy with family and I made a promise to Sam as well. He pouted at the family outing because he's gonna miss it. "I will not be left out too many more times...I'm gonna remedy that." We stood at the door holding each other not wanting to let go.

As I lie in bed relaxing Ms. Cora knocks and enters bringing me a cup of tea. "Miss Dominique I'm just checking on you, how are you?" "Ya know deep down lately." I sat up as she handed me the tea. Ms. Cora thank you I'm better a lot better. "Good I'm glad and I know I am of no relation but I feel comfortable in saying that mothafucka Jordan creeps me the hell out." "Lookin' suspect and shit it may not be my place but you and yours are my concern just be careful hell." My eyes got big as I sat up even higher. Ms. Cora have you been talkin' to my Momma about him? "No Miss Dominique, I've been around long enough to know we have to watch folks...all company ain't good company." I got up and stirred slowly about the room thinking my Momma damn near said the same thing. I sipped some tea. Well I can say I don't wanna have anything to do with him. He didn't even… "Show up at the funeral?" "I know Miss Dominique I pay attention and if I do say so myself he has an agenda of some sort, I'm no expert." "I may be wrong." "Just watch his ass." Will do Ms. Cora will do.

Before returning to school we, the kids and I, Momma, Auntie Etta and Ms. Cora will enjoy a week at Hye'raygo Bay one of the world's largest indoor water parks. Our rooms were Hawaiian style. Drinks (of any kind) served in freshly carved pineapples we wore lai's, grass skirts, the whole sha-bang. We skyped with Bryce and while skyping he showed up at the door of our room...surprised the hell outta me! Momma knew though, she thinks she's slick. I love it! I had missed him like crazy. (He stayed for 2 days then back to LA).

GOOD OLE FUN

I got the kids settled at Momma Lynn's I'm gonna meet Sam this afternoon...

We met at the gym, worked up a mean sweat, showered there. Stopped by Kroger to grab a couple of items for a beast of a salad that we'll be making back at her place. Of course, we bought gelato her favorite is salted caramel and I'm mad over pistachio. I measured ¼ cup of the pistachio to eat then I thought...ayyye let me take a walk on the wild side and have ½ a cup. Back when we were dating Sam purchased the King of Queens DVD collection (one my favorite's aside The Golden Girls) we sat and watched several episodes. Sam's a delight.

Topic of one of our little talks was Bryce. "I swear Purp at Pierre's homegoing Bryce was holding onto you like I would've been.' "Is he in love with you?" Yes. We are in love with each other. "As you know I love the ground you walk on and don't wanna see you with anything but a smile on your face." "You and those beautiful babies." "I am truly concerned about you guys' well-being and happiness." "So, are you guys thinking about marriage?" Oh my gosh Sam... I hadn't thought about that but hey it's an option. "I'll give you away even though it would about kill me." "Nonetheless love is love." Aww Samantha, thank you so much! I love you and the mere thought of you being willing to do that for me is a blessing. I am very happy to have you in my life and I would not change that for anything. "Neither would I." We fell asleep watching Nights of Rodanthe.

Before leaving to go home the next afternoon…

Sam and I took a brisk walk after breakfast and during our walk I talked with Bryce.

Momma and Ms. Cora had a surprise for me when I got home. Peeled grapes and cubed strawberries along with a masseuse. These women are awesome! Ma knows exactly what I like. Ms. Cora gettin' hip. After my massage, I skyped Bryce from practically every room in the house. I'm in love with this man and I don't care what anyone has to say about it.

Jordan called and texted several times. I didn't acknowledge him at all. He fucked up and the timing was perfect. I appreciate it, him revealing his true character and putting his "representative" on reserve. His actions or shall I say inaction left the "wondering" in the wind. During a tender and crucial time for my family and I, this bastard didn't have the decency to call me. He can kiss my ass in its entirety.

CHAPTER 5

School is back underway and all is well with the kids. I informed the counselor as well as the social worker at the school about their dad. So far so good. They are coping better than I expected. I know that distraction helps but I don't want them to keep questions, worries or concerns to themselves. I keep reassuring them.

Aunt Etta is saying that her neighbors have been working her last nerve for a couple of months now and if the offer still stands she wants to sell most of her things (her small business included) and move in. Yes!! I thought this would've come sooner she took long enough. I loved the idea beforehand. Momma had the option of living in the house within our home (the basement) her response was, "Why would I do that and I have all of this?" I can't blame her. Three women I admire in the house with me...this is a blessing. A curse to because the good cookin' and eatin' I'm gonna endure over the years will make me gain a ton.

Law Office
Of
Chandler, Danske and Rawls

Our schedules have been the total opposite of one another and today we find ourselves at the firm at the same time. Bryce had been in my office most of the morning and this afternoon we're going to meet Randolph Morrison (the P.I.) he would like me to see a video clip from the gas station where Pierre' was killed.

Bryce: Morrison says that the clip is just a little fuzzy but after speaking with him I do not want you to view the clip in its entirety. I wish you didn't have to do this at all but it's a must. He told me that a glimpse of the killer's face can be seen and I would like for you to take-a-look at that point...ok?

Sure baby, I replied nervously.

As he held me I buried my face in his chest. When he said ok...I looked. The killer wore a dark brown t-shirt and jeans. He may have been wearing black or dark blue sneakers it was hard to tell. Brown complexion, hair pulled back into a ponytail, some sort of circular lookin' tattoo on his left arm and he stood close to six feet ...maybe. My heart was dropped as I was looking at this bastard. He took someone precious from us! I'd kill 'em my damn self!

The clip was posted on the news off and on for several weeks...it went viral on social media. No one came forward. It was like this guy was a ghost that came into town for the sole purpose of killing my kid's daddy. The whole ordeal and the process of waiting had become very frustrating to say the least.

Speaking of the kids they want to spend most of their winter break with Momma Lynn which is great. I want them to. They need their grandma just as much as she needs them. I keep trying to encourage her about the ongoing investigation although deep down I was becoming discouraged. We must lift one another up and we do just that.

THE HOLIDAYS HAVE PAST (Sombering, Humbling and Reflective) ...

Enjoying relationships whether familial, personal or professional. Suffering a tremendous loss while regaining strength and focus. Releasing "friends", foes/fucks. Learning it is ok to forgive but not forget. Otherwise...what would the lesson be? Welcoming new-found love with open arms as well as rekindling a friendship or two...

AWAITING SPRING TO BE SPRUNG...

I am on my way to meet Sam at the Shrimp Hut. She and Tiffani have been hitting it off and she wants to "talk" to me about her. To get my approval I guess. It's funny because I felt irritated by the idea of her mentioning her crush to me. Ugggh! It's not like I have feelings for her. Or do I? No. But being with her wouldn't be morally correct nor socially acceptable. That's what I think or at least this is what I was raised to think and that's the reason I stopped seeing her. Ma would disown me too... I guess...I don't know. Nonetheless Bryce has my heart.

Before getting out of the car at the Shrimp Hut I began to feel sick and phoned Sam. She came to greet me and as we entered and while walking to our table I got lightheaded and couldn't hardly stand the smell of the seafood. We got to the table, sat then I took a few sips of water. As soon as I felt a little better I stood up and when I did I felt faint again leaning on Sam. She got me the hell out of there. While outside taking in a little fresh air I called Bryce and he was immediately worried. Sam and I both had to calm him down. All I was thinkin' was...I want my Mommy. I left my car at the restaurant and Sam drove me home.

We stopped and bought some soup. As she drove I ate and asked her to talk to me about Tiffani. "She's an English Professor at Dentworth University, we have a lot in common, not more than you and I but enough." Does she lighten your load? "Yes, she makes my day in every way Purp." Please Sam go for it. I want you to have the smile that you have on your face right now until the end of time. What's her nationality? "Quit playin' Purp you know I loves me a sista." I know just thought I'd ask. We both giggled.

Sam walks me to the door and sees me in. Momma spoke to her in a friendly manner and smiled. That was strange or different I thought. Sam and I hug each other tightly. She says, "You think…". What? I asked. "Oh, never mind I'll chat with you a little later." Ok sweetums. I walk over to Momma and kiss her cheeks. Mommy, Mommy…I DO NOT FEEL GOOD! She held me while rubbing and kissing my forehead. "Bryce called just before you got here and he should be pulling up any minute." "We are gonna get to the bottom of this." My Mother and my lover chatting it up how cute I thought. I dozed off for a minute while lying under Momma.

Ms. Cora made me some Chamomile tea with ginger. I turned the television on to this flea market show it was interesting. Moms and I were diggin' it. I could smell Bryce as he came into the house. I wanted to jump into his arms but I felt so weak. He spoke to Ma and Ms. Cora the he removed his loosened tie, unbuttons his shirt, removes his shoes, kisses me and then he sits on the floor in front of Ma and myself. He turned to look at me and says, "Aww my poor baby you look pale." No fever, no chills (sighing) I vomited a little a day or two ago maybe it's a lil stomach bug/flu. Uggh I just don't know.

Momma and Aunt Etta are running out to the store to pick up a few things for Auntie's living space. Ms. Cora decided to stay at the house and in doing so she made me her mystery cure all soup. That was nice of her I thought. When Momma got up I rolled onto the floor with Bryce and he held me. Moments later I got a piggyback ride to the bedroom. He sat me down on the bed and went to run some bath water. Lookin' damn good in his boxers I must say. I love him so much and am grateful we have been brought together. As the water ran he turned some light jazz on and proceeded to undress me while he talked briefly about work and hopes that the investigation regarding Pierre' starts to look promising.

He leads me into the bathroom turns the water off and kisses me. It was breathtaking and as if it were our very first time. We held each other for a moment. He helped me into the tub and then followed. He began kissing the nape of my neck and says to me, "Baby I think you're pregnant." Those words sent a warm and tingly chill down my spine. Why, what, why...what makes you say that baby? "Well the symptoms you've been having and you did not have a period last month." Wait a minute...I did, didn't I? "No baby you didn't...I pay close attention to you woman." "You're pale now because you've vomited twice in the last couple weeks or less... morning sickness is the culprit."

Well damn I don't think I had period last month now that I think about it. My skirts have been feeling a little snug. Hmmm... The time for my cycle is approaching and I do not feel moody like I usually would. Maybe I am pregnant. Oh my! "To resolve our curiosity, I bought a pregnancy test." As he bathes me I start to feel woozy...he helps me out of the tub. I tinkle on the stick and then Bryce helps me to bed because I am quite dizzy. I lie there in the fetal position as he gently massages and kisses me. Bryce goes to the bathroom and without looking at the test-strip he brings it for us both to see...he turns it over and… "Yes, we're pregnant!!"

And to think being pregnant hadn't crossed my mind. Telling my family was a cinch. It came as no surprise to everyone except me. We told Bryce's parents who live in Hawaii and his sister Melanie who lives in Paris (part-time) via video chat. They were all ecstatic.

THE BEGINNING

Two weeks after learning about the pregnancy Bryce asked me to marry him. It was very romantic and a memory that I will cherish:

As our carriage ride came to an end Emily King appeared and serenaded her hit "You and I" to me as Bryce proposed. (Our eyes met when this song was playing at a picnic that was given by the firm approximately 2 years ago. I have often said that I would sing this a someone's wedding). Crying like a baby I said yes...we eloped in the Cayman Islands.

A large ceremony will be held after the baby is born. I didn't tell Momma we had gotten married she'd kill the both of us. It was so hard not telling her that I am MRS. DOMINIQUE P. CHANDLER!!! Beaming from ear to ear all the time. Our witnesses were my sister in law Melanie, Vicki (yes, I know), Bryce's best friends Anton and Terrance. The view was breathtakingly beautiful with an array of colorful flowers within the decor coral, cream, and purple. That was OUR wedding.

Vicki and I had gotten a little closer...she asked for a chance, I gave it and since then she has been very true to me and mine. Her man Chris works with Jordan. It didn't bother me because Chris must make living. I still hadn't met him. Perhaps he'll make himself available for the wedding. One condition of my friendship with Vicki is that she never mentions Jordan to me or my family. She expresses regret to me for introducing us. I told her that she cannot control anyone else's actions or inactions.

Side note:

I had not heard much from Sam. I assume her girlfriend did not want us to keep in touch and that hurts. I love that woman she's near and dear to my heart.

My prince and princess cannot wait until our bundle of joy arrives. Their relationship with Bryce has grown to be very strong. He helps them with their homework, goes on field trips, cooks with them (some food edible and some not lol), attends sporting activities and car pools…he's an awesome dad. After we got married I gave him custodial rights to my Demi and Denim.

My husband no longer wanted the penthouse he shared with his ex-wife therefore he put it on the market and it wasn't there for long. It was sold within a couple of months. We will reside at the home I purchased but when the baby is about a year old we will go a little larger. Bryce and I have discussed the foundation/layout plan and surrounding areas for our new home. Which will include a guest house suitable for Aunt Etta and Ms. Cora. Momma vows to never leave the main house and again I cannot blame her. The children are excited to be able to have some input on how their rooms will be designed. Momma Lynn stays actively involved with the kids. She's crazy about her grandbabies and has been since day one.

My due date is August 10th (a little under two weeks away) ...

It's sweltering out here! My family and I are at the supermarket and I swear from the car to the entrance I lost a pound and I got out at the door!! Finally, some cold air. Bryce and his googly eyes makes my fat swollen pregnant ass feel like I'm the only one he sees.

Bryce: (whispers) Hey wife of mine, my beautiful butterfly... (then he plants a huge wet one on me and of course I return the favor). I know what we need is there anything you'd like in particular?

Just my delectable husband... oh and some Italian ice. We stood there gazing at one another and giggling.

Momma: What did you just say?

I want some Italian ice… (she gave me a sassy smirk). My Momma…a smirk?? I bet she heard me say husband and oh well I'm gonna play dumb.

Bryce and the kids walked up ahead of Ma and I to the freezer aisle. As I approached that section it got colder and colder…feeling damn good. All -of- a -sudden, I felt a warm sensation. I grasped the shopping cart looked down…my water broke! Momma yelled for Bryce. He and the kids came running. Everyone was in a panic except me. It was cute seeing them all look and act a lil edgy but it's time to get out of there.

We were met at the hospital by the gang. Aunt Etta, Momma Lynn, Ms. Cora, Melanie, Vicki, Anton, Terrance and Bryce's parents (they had flown in a week ago) and would you believe it Sam!! (I later found out that Vicki reached out to her). Four hours later I gave birth to an eight pound three ounce twenty-one-inch baby boy. Bryce insists his name be Donovan. I was ecstatic and crying but I felt like our son's name should be Bryce and there you have it…

Bryce Donovan Chandler. A few weeks later we announced his Godparents Sam and Anton. I thought Momma was gonna lose it and slap the shit out of Vicki because during the announcement gathering she interrupted saying, "I had asked to be his God-mom." I don't know why she blurted that out. She had asked to be the baby's God-mom during my pregnancy and I told her no. Therefore, I do not understand why interruption or the perplexed look. In a rather upset state Vicki says, "And you...bitch I'm the reason why you're even here (pointing at Sam)." Sam jumped up and shoved the shit out of her... shouting, "Yo' wanna be best friend ass... not today ya hoe!" Terrance had to keep Sam from whooping Vicki's ass and Melanie had to defer Momma. I thought really Vicki...really? You are partially back in my good graces and this is what you do? Back your ass down before it gets handled.

Over the summer the kids participated at camp for just three weeks. They were worried about their big ole pregnant momma and rightfully so. A few times a week I assist them with bathing their little brother before bedtime. They have taken on their roles as older siblings with pride I must say. Momma and Ms. Cora are a great help it's a blessing. Aunt Etta hasn't been around much lately. She has been gambling a bit too much Momma says. I sure as hell hope she gets that shit together. Momma Lynn had been travelling to California and felt no sincerity from her family about Pierre' with-the-exception of an aunt of hers that used to babysit Pierre' when

Momma Lynn resided in California years and years ago. Periodic leads on Pierre's killer led to nowhere. We aren't giving up...that's not an option.

Three months later...

Christmas was beautiful...the smiles, laughter, cinnamon/pine scented air, the love and the absolute joy of giving!! Baby Bryce is getting chunky and breast milk is to thank for that as well as the goulash Momma and Ms. Cora feeds him. He's a little cutie, grayish blue eyes, full little lips, dark brown hair and he has a caramel complexion (like his momma). He favors us all in one way or another. He got a few plush toys for Christmas. Everyone and I mean everyone was pleased with their gifts.

The kids have prepared to spend time with Momma Lynn and want their little brother to join them. Momma said it'd be ok because she'd be going as well in order to help. They will be leaving some time tomorrow. I received a call from a heartbroken Sam. Come to find out Sam's girlfriend was cheating with some dude she met online. Initially Sam didn't have any indication then it became obvious. She also stated no one could ever keep her away from me. "I backed up to let you live Purp and it almost killed me." "Although I knew there was no hope for us...I held onto a maybe." We were able to catch up a great deal.

It was a bitterly cold wintery night....

I had just finished nursing the baby and got him comfy in his crib. I was about to enter Momma's room to tell her goodnight but she was having a heated discussion...more like an argument with Aunt Etta. I'm not typically an eavesdropper but I could not believe my ears. Aunt Etta was loud saying something like, "Well...it doesn't matter got-damnit, I'll ask her..."

Momma says, "No Etta don't come worrying my baby with that!" Then she burst into tears, "Etta what is wrong with you?" "It has to be more than gambling...yes...yes she is!!!" "She IS my baby!!"

Somewhat muffled but audible...

Aunt Etta: Well we'll see about that...yo ass ain't got not right....

Momma (cries): I have every right!

I could not take it any longer, I burst into her room...Momma! Momma! Why are you crying? What the hell is going on? "It's Etta baby." I gathered that. What the f... what is her problem? Momma was shaking I held her very close and tight. "I... I'm not your birth mother...Etta is." I held her even tighter as I wept. Yes, you ARE my Mother and I don't give a damn what no one has to say. "Let me tell you what happened baby." I listened while continuing to hold her.

She explained that Aunt Etta got pregnant by one of her superior officers who was married…

"So, in order to continue with her career, she gave you to me right after you were born and signed over her rights." "Ultimately she was honorably discharged because of her alcohol problem not on merit...baby Purp I love you with all my h…" I know Momma you don't have to tell me that, I'll kill for you...you ARE my MOMMA nothing or no one can change that. We talked, reminisced, laughed, cried and held each other. She fell asleep. I silenced her phone. After tucking her in I headed to the living room. Bryce and the big babies were on the couch and they were half asleep. "Hey, my beautiful butterfly we drank hot chocolate, chatted and after about 30 minutes they started to drift off." "You look disturbed love...the babies told me you were in Ma's room, I didn't want to disturb you guys, is everything alright?" (Sighing) Let's get them to bed baby and we'll talk.

Dimmed lights, fireplace turned on in the bedroom....

While taking a soak together I gave Bryce the skinny. Neither one of us could understand why Aunt Etta would do this...bring any of this up now. At this point it doesn't even matter. No one mistreats my Momma. No fuckin' body. She has been through hell and high water for me and I'll be damned if any bitch is gonna worry her. Point, blank, period. I needed to vent and was glad Bryce allowed me to. We are in agreement that Aunt Etta has to leave and the kids cannot go anywhere with her. After getting out of the tub I called Ms. Cora to let her know. She was just on her way in to check on baby Bryce and to get herself a snack. As we lay snug and cozy I emailed the school to inform them that Aunt Etta is off limits there I sent an attachment to their camps as well. They're on break but while the thought is fresh...I will also call and email once again when they return to school.

Bryce massages my tense shoulders, ahhhh... I turned around to kiss him. The passion is mystical and I love it. I straddle him backwards in order to eagerly feast upon one another...in sync lathering his dick with my wet warm mouth as he tastes the sweet nectar of my pussy ever so gently then the rotation of his tongue turns savage ...he's slappin' and grabbin' my ass cheeks while I'm giving that dick the business... we clutch... I experienced an orgasm that was cosmic. Savoring the nut from his spout allowed us to quench one another's thirst...shit had me almost crying. Damn and he's all mine.

During my pregnancy Bryce, Melanie, Vicki and I were planning a New Year's Day party but those plans have changed. There was going to be a gathering at our house but in light of Aunt Etta's craziness maybe another time. Now we will focus on building our new home and the wedding.

UNDER CONSTRUCTION

We vacationed at our home in Florida over the summer with family and a few friends. And while there we visited Disney World of course. Toward the end of summer my husband and I flew to France with two couples. Vicki and Chris were invited but as usual he would be tied up...it never fails. Bryce and I tried to convince Vicki to join us but she was really upset therefore she declined. Honestly, I don't think he's loyal to her but hey...I'll be a shoulder if need be. I hope it doesn't come to that. Sometimes I think Chris feels bothered by the fact that if it hadn't been for Jordan being his friend none of us would be in this awkward situation. Either way Vicki appears to be in love and in that case, I'll remain happy for her.

We have a wedding rehearsal coming up and Sam kept her word to give me away...I love her. I truly do. She's a great woman and an even better friend. Bryce and I were debating on where our wedding should take place and decided to have it at the firm's hall where seminars and such are held. It will be more than enough space but space that'll be needed for the children too. The executive dining area is extravagant and with the expertise of Mel and Vicki I know the decor will be magnificent.

On another note Aunt Etta tried contacting Bryce at the office. She wanted money and tried to get him to understand that he's her son in law...that situation was rectified immediately. Hell, I was willing to talk to her but she told my husband that Momma had done brainwashed me and that I wouldn't understand where she was coming from so on and so forth. I'm not even gonna entertain her ass. I'm done.

By the end of next summer our new home will no longer be under construction. (Hopefully)

WEDDED BLISS

At the end of the aisle stands a man I do not want to live without...

A cream and coral sheer/silk spun gown with lace that hugs my curves, exquisite yet slightly provocative with a seven-foot train to follow. The gentle yet strong way Sam held my arm as she walked me down the aisle to meet the love of my life was felt within the depths of my soul. The hug and ever so lightly peck on the forehead from her gave me a feeling of gratefulness for her even more so. The once said vows were repeated and we both added a word at the end. An explanation for the word(s) will be given at the reception.

Sam and Vicki mean mugged one another a couple times. I hope they can get past this...either way this isn't the time nor the place for their shenanigans. There were many in attendance (approximately a hundred or maybe more) our immediate families of course with- the-exception of Aunt Etta. My neighbor Mrs. Johnston, her husband and the kids, several coworkers who brought significant others and or their children. Anton and Terrance (best man and one of the groomsmen) along with their fiancee's and their mom's (the guys mom's) who have been like family to Bryce. A couple of

Momma's friends, Melanie's bff came and brought his fiancee'. The bff Nathan aka Nate thought he knew me from somewhere. I could not recall ever meeting him. Senior partner Rawls was in attendance with his two sons and daughter (all three are attorneys) his son Liam brought his wife and two children. Mr. Rawls and Ms. Cora seemed to be hitting it off. A cousin here and there along with a friend or three of other friends. All which were welcome.

Bryce detached the train from my gown then took me front line and center on the dance floor. With mic in hand while looking into my eyes he says, "Solid as your focus, colorful as your beauty, zany as your personality, wings that flutter such as my heart every time I look at you and carefree as the wind." "Butterfly." He gave me the mic and while gazing into those enticing blue eyes I said, two people, two hearts...one "Soul" and those were the words we chose. "Butterfly-Soul."

A few toasts were given and delightful they were. An entire wall on the dancefloor were slides from days leading up to and during the wedding. A man that looked awfully familiar asked to have the first dance. I glanced over at Momma and she was crying. As I figured it was Uncle Eddie. Suave and debonair, broad shoulders about six- foot three looking like the older version of what Donovan would have looked like. Our dance was pleasingly graceful. Uncle Eddie whispered to me, "There was no way on earth I was gonna miss my one and only niece's wedding...absolutely not." "I love you baby Purp and I always will…" I love you too Uncle Eddie…

Soon thereafter everyone hit the dancefloor. I shook and grinded this ass all on my husband and he didn't miss a beat. We ate, drank, laughed, making some lovable and precious memories. Karen, one of the firm's corporate executive secretaries caught the bouquet. Our honeymoon took place in Hawaii where my in-laws reside.

My contract at the firm is long over and presently I am undecided about employment. I could return to the firm but there isn't an urgent need for me to work at this time. My husband wants me to stop working and pursue my PHD (I've given that some though in the past). I enjoy writing poetry and going to spoken word in the D. During this time off I will do just that... write and perform perhaps...it's a great release for me. With support from my husband, Momma, Momma Lynn and Ms. Cora all will be well.

My prince and princess are doing exceptionally well academically and with everything that has transpired in our lives they're balancing in daily living also. We keep them occupied and there's also down time for us as a family. Besides our regular schedules... every Wednesday, Saturday and Sunday we either read, watch movies, participate in spiritual awakenings and or simply talk without any distractions. ALL of us appreciate those days, Ms. Cora included. Bryce the kids and I went to see Sesame Street on ice and in a few weeks, all of us will be going to the circus.

In my opinion one of life's most important gifts are memories.

A few weeks later, on the phone with Uncle Eddie...

Aunt Etta reached out to him but not in a welcoming manner. She wanted him to try and disrupt our wedding per se. "I didn't pay her any mind, I wanted to know when and where the wedding was taking place in order to be there unbeknown to her," Uncle Eddie stated. He went on to say, "Etta has issues...always has, if it wasn't her drinking it was something else or another." "Ella told me that you know about Etta and personally Baby Purp the best thing Etta has ever done was give you to Ella." I know that as well Uncle Eddie. "Just call me Unc", he replied. We went on to talk for hours.

APPROXIMATELY 18 MONTHS LATER...

Despite efforts driven with hope of Pierre's killer being brought to justice the flame has dimmed. Momma Lynn as well as the rest of us try to remain positive regardless. My babies try their best to help Grandma Lynn cope (lil Bryce keeps both grannies on their toes). Momma and Ms. Cora make a great team. They are very resourceful when it comes to children and maintaining a household. I am forever grateful and indebted to them. There were delays with the development of our home which is finally completed. A few inspections and we'll be good to go. We will soon be gearing up for our move and we are all super excited!!

I was getting to know my Uncle a little more as well as one of my cousins, Ahnjella (a spitting image of myself) who over several years kept in touch with some people from Detroit including Vicki which she failed to mention. This enlightenment wasn't expected yet not surprising.

Oddly Jordan still has been contacting me and just as recent as two days ago. I didn't even mention it to Bryce. I had been ignoring him but there are some things he says that make me wonder until he speaks ill of my husband. He'd say things like, "Dominique, please hear me out...you don't know him as well as you think you do." I don't know if this was an attempt to gain good graces with me or what but I told him that Bryce is my husband and he needs to stop contacting me. He replied, "Oh, I know he is and I hate it for many reasons." Name me one reason why Jordan. "Please... let me see you face to face I know my previous actions/inactions makes me unworthy of your time but I swear to you I had my reasons." "You deserve a better man than me and the one you have."

Jordan's words weren't just words it was the way he spoke. I "felt" him in a bizarre sort of way. Some of his words were heartfelt as well as bone chilling. Either way I heard sincerity in his voice which terrified me. I asked myself why has Jordan gone through several failed attempts to connect with me over the last couple years? I don't know but I am ready to get this over with therefore I will meet with him and hear him out.

ON THE PHONE WITH JORDAN…

I must meet with inspectors at my new home the middle of next week…

"I know Dominique."

Really? How so?

"There is so much you are unaware of and it's unfair."

"I was falling for you and…. "

"Give me a location, date, time and I'm there."

Umm... Emagine Museum next Tuesday at noon.

"Gotcha."

My mind was running rampant. The fiery, heart-pounding, mind boggling and horrid thoughts of the unknown were inescapable. My imagination consumed me making Tuesday seem very far away. While in fact it'll be here in five days. I do not know what to expect to hear from Jordan but it doesn't sound good.

I reached out to Sam and made her promise not to tell my whereabouts when I go to meet Jordan. I wanted to make someone aware that I can trust. I know that I can trust my Mom but with the way she worries she would probably tell Bryce and I don't want that. Although Bryce has never, ever given me a reason to distrust him I owe it to myself to hear what Jordan has to say in order to ease my thunderous thoughts.

Thoughts that have me somewhat distracted. Bryce asked me was I alright...why do you ask I replied. "I have been talking to you about the case I have on Monday and I will return home Tuesday evening and you didn't say anything...ya know the cute things you normally say or do." "What's going on?" My mind is just a little preoccupied. "Why Butterfly?" Aunt Etta is trying to work my nerve. I had to verbally assassinate her and it gave me some relief but the mystery still remains as to why on earth is she continuing to try and disrupt my or my family's happiness. Just evil. "Aww Butterfly, I'm sorry, is there anything I can do?" No baby I'll be fine. Being here and listening is more than enough. Let me gather your things as well as a pair of my underwear. "What color?" There's no need to worry your pretty lil head about that.

The evening turned out to be rather pleasing. We ate, went for a walk, returned home, watched a movie in our theater room and lastly saw the kids off to bed. We're expecting Ma and Ms.Cora to get back a little later. About three times a month they attend dance and art classes followed by a cocktail or two. They are chauffeured of course.

Bryce and I went out back to skinny dip and snatched one another's souls while doing so. His back is scratched up and my ass cheeks are welted. Both of us have bite marks.

Yeah, we "fuck" some shit up regularly. S&M is a must have… I love it and am glad he understands as well as complying, otherwise we couldn't be together.

The following morning...

Demi and Denim got ready for school while lil Bryce and I made breakfast. Afterward we saw Daddy off then our driver took the babies to school.

LONG AWAITED TUESDAY

My phone startled me at three thirty in the morning.

It's Sam's ringtone...

"Purp I'm sorry to wake you." It's fine are you ok? "Yes, I had to call because I have been tossin' n turnin' from eerie nightmarish thoughts." "Later today I want to be nearby when you meet with that dude just in case." And you can Sam, I have no problem with that. None whatsoever. We talked for about an hour then she drifted off to sleep. Poor Sam is anxious. I am, too. Not about Jordan though but about what he has to say.

Momma, Ms. Cora and I had coffee and toast after the kids went off to school. Lil Bryce is eager to go to "swkool" as he puts it. He is adorable and tries to help with any and everything around the house despite being in the terrible two-phase...which will be ending soon. Time flies.

As we were watching the news Momma asked me what were my plans for the day. "Are you gonna work on some more of your writing for the club Baby Purp?" I am Momma, right after I get back. I've gotta meet an acquaintance around eleven or so. "Oh ok...who?" Melanie's bff. "Nate?"

Yes Ma. Ya know he is getting married and wanted me to help him choose a few patterns to run by his fiance'. "That's odd." How so? (She laughs and responds...) "Well he didn't ask me for my expertise." (I don't think I've ever lied to my Mother...ever and that did not feel good at all.) I'll tell her sooner than later. I must.

It's 11:30 a.m... Emagine Museum just opened its doors...

I'm sitting in the cafe' area awaiting Jordan. I've called Sam for the third time and still no response. She probably overslept. I started to drop by her place but I thought her ass would have gotten up by now and besides I'm more than eager to get this shit over with. I honestly hope this is no bullshit attempt on Jordan's behalf to try to "get" me for that ship has sailed. I must admit I was feeling something for him that was until he jumped ship when I needed him the most.

The time is 11:55 a.m.

Here comes Sam, we nod then I call her cell phone. He isn't here yet. I will give him until a quarter after then...

I look up and there he is. Jordan looks buff as hell. Wow! Any way let me focus on the purpose of our meeting.

Jordan: Hello Mrs. Dominique how are you?

Very anxious otherwise I am fine.

Jordan: You are radiant.

You look good yourself Jordan.

How have you been?

Jordan: For quite some time I was stressed almost beyond repair.

???Really???

Jordan: Yes. I told you over the phone that I had fallen for you...it wasn't my job that came between us. Not solely anyway.

I grabbed his hand...what's going on Jordan? "First let me start from a couple of months ago." "As you know Dominique my job can keep me occupied between a few states." "Anyhow somewhere along the line I missed a few pieces of mail and there is a video I want you to see." "It gives further confirmation of what I was going to show and tell you regardless." "I want you to relax as well as brace yourself, can I come sit closer to you?" Yes. He pulled out earbuds and his laptop then inserted a hard drive. "Ok beautiful I'm here."

"Just watch and listen I will do the same with you." I glanced over to Sam and nervously responded...ok. Jordan held my hand. I was just barely able to recognize the woman on the screen but it was Bryce's ex-wife Lisa…

"Hello Dominique, we were never formally introduced. My name is Lisa Chandler and if you are watching this, it means I am no longer living…"

PAUSE.

TO BE CONTINUED……

Made in the USA
Middletown, DE
13 February 2023

24002595R00064